D0550791

WITHDRAWN

Treloar College

FROM STOCK

R07643Y2386

Text copyright © Anthony Masters 1998
Illustrations copyright © Alan Marks 1998

First published in Great Britain in 1998 by
Macdonald Young Books

Reprinted in 2000 by Hodder Wayland,
an imprint of Hodder Children's Books

Hodder Children's Books
A division of Hodder Headline
338 Euston Road
London NW1 3BH

The right of Anthony Masters to be identified as the author
and Alan Marks the illustrator of this Work has been
asserted by them in accordance with the
Copyright, Designs and Patents Act 1988

Designed and Typeset by Backup Creative Services, Dorset DT10 1DB
Printed and bound in Belgium by Proost International Book Production

British Library Cataloguing in Publication Data available

ISBN: 0 7500 2467 4

ANTHONY MASTERS

PHANTOMS IN
THE FOG

Illustrated by Alan Marks

HODDER
Wayland

an imprint of Hodder Children's Books

Chapter One

Matt Hardy walked slowly up the dark and crumbling staircase of the empty house. He could feel rotten wood beneath his feet and smell raw, shut-in damp.

Something scampered in the darkness. Was it a rat? Cobwebs brushed Matt's face and his torch picked out a black, hairy spider crawling up the banisters. He shuddered.

Outside, Andrew waited, wishing he hadn't dared Matt to spend a whole half-hour in Marsh House.

Dense fog clung to the marsh, occasionally shifting to reveal a couple of sheep and some spiky bushes.

The old ruined house had belonged to the Hardy family for generations. But no one had lived there for years and Matt's parents now owned a sheep farm nearby.

Andrew had always been curious about the old place. As he gazed up at it, the fog swirled round its windows, making them look like staring eyes.

Matt was on the landing now. The bare boards creaked beneath his feet.

Years ago, when Matt's Great-uncle Henry was a child, he had died on the marsh trying to rescue his sister Gwen.

Tonight was the anniversary of their deaths and that's why Andrew had dared him. The legend said that on the anniversary of their deaths, Henry and Gwen Hardy were always seen together, looking out of the windows of Marsh House. Matt wished he had never taken up the challenge.

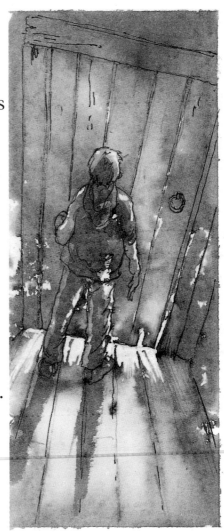

Matt suddenly saw a faint light flickering from underneath a door at the far end of the landing. He came to an abrupt halt and his heart started hammering.

No one Matt knew had actually seen the ghosts. Was he going to be the first?

Slowly Matt began to move on again, his hand shaking so much that he nearly dropped the torch.

Chapter Two

A strand of slithering fog parted briefly
to reveal the notice outside Marsh House.
Andrew shivered, feeling guilty and afraid.
He should have known that Matt would
take up the dare. Matt always had to
prove himself.

Andrew had been jealous of him ever since Matt had been made striker on their school football team. Andrew had been dropped.

Andrew looked down at his watch. The dare had another fifteen minutes to run.

Then Andrew saw something move. Was that a figure running out of the front door of Marsh House? Had Matt lost his nerve already?

"Matt?" yelled Andrew. "Time's not up yet!"

But the boy didn't seem to hear, although he was running in his direction.

The strands of fog parted again and Andrew froze. The boy was tall and thin with a shock of blond hair. This wasn't Matt. As the figure came nearer, Andrew felt a cold chill. He could see through it.

Andrew couldn't move. It was as if he had been turned to stone.

At the last moment, he used all his will-power, turned and burst into a stumbling run.

The light streamed out from underneath the door of the room at the end of the landing. Matt stood there, shivering, not wanting to touch the handle. He kept staring down. The light definitely wasn't made by electricity. It was more of a glow.

Matt knew he had to turn the door handle. Slowly, very slowly, he reached out and then let go with a cry of terror. The handle was so icy cold that it had almost burnt his hand.

Matt turned round and gazed down the landing. He could hardly see. It was as if the fog had suddenly filled the old house.

Chapter Three

Andrew ran for the Hardys' farm, which was the nearest place of safety. As he banged on the door he kept looking over his shoulder, but all he could see was the fog, thickening into a huge cloud behind him.

Matt's older sister Laura opened the door.

"Matt's not here." Laura had never really liked Andrew.

"I saw a boy who wasn't there."

"Are you trying to be funny?" Laura was obviously annoyed.

"I could see right through him. You've got to help me. I dared Matt to stay in Marsh House for half an hour and he's still there." Andrew was obviously panic-stricken and Laura realized there was something terribly wrong.

"I'll get my coat," she said, gazing out at the deepening fog. "That place is dangerous."

Matt tried the handle again. This time it wasn't so freezing cold. He pulled, and the door opened unwillingly. Then he gasped in fear and bewilderment.

Matt was gazing into a boy's bedroom. It was very old-fashioned but, unlike the rest of Marsh House, was still furnished.

He switched off his torch because the strange glow picked out a narrow bed, a small desk and shelves full of leather-bound books. There was a spinning top in one corner and a chess set on a small table, but when he reached out to touch the chess pieces, Matt's hand went straight through them. He tried again with one of the books and the same thing happened.

Shaking, Matt stared around him, noticing that there was a slight haze round the edges of the room that seemed to be edging nearer.

He turned towards the half-open door, but it suddenly slammed in his face. When Matt tried the handle, once again the cold was so great that his hand stuck to it painfully. With difficulty he pulled it away, leaving his flesh sore and smarting.

Chapter Four

"I can't see a thing," moaned Andrew.

"I know the way," snapped Laura.
"I thought Matt was at football practice.
You're both so stupid. He could have
fallen through any of those rotten floors."
Laura broke into a run, charging over
the uneven boggy ground, heading for
Marsh House.

"Wait for me!" yelled Andrew.

"You'll have to catch up!"

But he couldn't and soon got left
behind. He was really scared. There was
no sign of Laura now, the fog seemed even
denser and when he shouted again there
was no reply.

Matt rattled and pulled at the handle. It wasn't so cold now, but even so the door still wouldn't open. Eventually he gave up. The fear pounded inside him and he went to the window. All Matt could see outside was a wall of fog.

Although the glass in most of the windows of Marsh House had long since broken, this one was intact. When Matt tried to pull the window down it wouldn't move. In desperation, Matt took off his shoe and tried to smash the glass, but it was too strong.

Then he saw something, someone, move in the fog outside. Dimly he could make out a girl. She was running. At first relief surged through Matt as he thought Laura had arrived to rescue him.

Then Matt realized that the shadowy figure wasn't Laura at all. The girl was wearing a long coat and a bonnet. Then the fog closed in again.

Chapter Five

Despite having lived on the marsh all her life, Laura had lost her way. Her sense of direction was usually good, but now it had completely deserted her.

Gazing round desperately, trying to pick out a familiar landmark, Laura saw a patch of bright green grass. With a surge of panic, she realized that she had wandered into one of the most dangerous parts of the marsh.

Laura knew she would have to tread carefully. If she didn't, she could sink and go on sinking just like her Great-aunt Gwen had done so many years ago.

Sick with fear, Matt pulled at the door as hard as he could. Then it opened so suddenly that he almost fell over. Somehow he managed to keep on his feet, switch on the torch and run back along the dark, cobweb-hung landing.

Matt didn't even try to be careful as he pounded down the rotten stairs. Several times he felt the surface crumble, but he hung on to the rickety banisters until he reached the hallway.

Matt dashed towards the front door and dragged it open. Gasping with relief he ran out into the night.

"Andrew?" Matt yelled. "Where are you?"

But there was no reply, and when he called again his words seemed eaten up by the hungry fog.

He's chickened out and gone home, Matt thought furiously. Well, he'd get him for that at school tomorrow.

Then he glanced back at Marsh House and his heart began to hammer again.

A boy had thrown open the bedroom window and was staring out. He had a mop of tousled blond hair and was calling a name over and over again.

"Gwen?" came the thin cry. "Where are you, Gwen?"

The figure of the boy began to shimmer and his voice started to fade until there was nothing left. A strand of fog drifted over the window and then Matt heard it slam shut. All he could hear now was a faint echo, and then he realized it was the distant hooting of an owl.

Laura was sinking and the mud was already well up over her knees. The more she struggled, the deeper she sank.

"Andrew!" she screamed. "Andrew! You've got to help me. I'm in the marsh. I'm going down. Help!"

But although Laura thought she heard a muffled cry it didn't come again, and soon she was up to her waist in mud and still sinking. "Help!" she cried desperately. "Someone help me."

Anxious to get home and not looking where he was going, Matt soon lost the path that he knew so well.

Within minutes he found himself surrounded by patches of boggy-looking ground and knew if he wasn't careful he could sink without trace. Then he heard someone crying out.

"Who is it?" Matt yelled as he tried to retrace his steps.

Suddenly, he heard the call again and forced himself to a halt, listening intently. Could it be Andrew? Or better still Laura?

"Henry," came the desperate voice. "Henry. You've got to help me. I'm sinking."

To his amazement Matt found that he was back on the path again. He heard footsteps pass him and felt a rush of bitterly cold air. But he could see no one.

"Gwen," came a thin shout from nearby. "Gwen. Where are you?"

"I'm over here, Henry," came the louder and even more desperate reply. "I'm over here and I'm sinking. The marsh is swallowing me up!"

Chapter Six

Matt heard the footsteps returning and felt another rush of cold air, this time even closer. Then he caught a glimpse of the boy again, his tangled hair soaked, his eyes wide with terror. He disappeared and there was a long silence that was broken by a despairing cry.

"I can't see you, Gwen. I can't see you."
There was a squelching, sucking sound
and the boy's thin voice screamed, "I'm
coming to get you!"

Then a familiar voice desperately cried
out Matt's name.

"Laura!" he yelled. "Where are you,
Laura?"

To his joy, her reply came at once. "I'm over here, Matt. You've got to get me out. I'm sinking."

Then he heard the squelching, sucking sound again. This time it was louder and nearer.

"Keep shouting!" Matt left the path and began to run towards the sound of his sister's voice. The squelching came again and he realized that this time he was making it himself as he began to wade into the bog.

The fog lifted slightly and Matt suddenly saw Laura. To his horror she was nearly up to her shoulders in the mud.

"Be careful where you tread," she yelled at him and he slowed down, walking more cautiously.

"Laura," came a faint cry which sounded as if it were a long way away. "Laura!"

It was Andrew, and Matt knew that if he came any nearer he would be in danger as well.

"It's Matt. I'm with her!" he shouted. "Stay away. Don't come in any further."

Matt lay flat on his stomach and reached out to try and grab his sister's hands. Laura stretched them towards him but the movement made her sink deeper. "Don't move. I'll come to you," Matt instructed.

"You can't," she said. "You'll only get sucked down."

However much he strained, Matt couldn't reach her. He moved a little nearer, but as he did so he felt the ground move beneath him and quickly edged back again.

Strong hands suddenly gripped Matt's
ankles so hard that his first reaction was to
kick out at them. But they held on and he
realized they must be Andrew's.

The grip tightened and he instinctively
moved forward until his stomach was
over the bog. Reaching out he grabbed
Laura's wrists.

Directly he had made contact with his sister, there was a sharp tugging on Matt's ankles and he felt himself being pulled backwards. For a moment Laura didn't budge. Then there was an oozing, sucking sound as slowly, very slowly, she began to come clear.

With a final squelch, Laura came out of the mud like a cork from a bottle, but the tugging on Matt's ankles didn't stop. Instead he was still being pulled backwards, but faster now until, gasping and shivering, Matt and Laura were both on firm ground.

Immediately the grip on Matt's ankles relaxed. He rolled over on to his back and saw, just above him, a shadow with thick blond hair. Matt froze.

Then the fog quickly became dense again, but to his amazement Matt saw that the glow which had been behind the door of the boy's bedroom was back, this time picking out a path through the marsh.

As they reached Marsh House on the
still glowing track, Andrew came running
up.

"What have—"

But Matt silenced him with a finger
to his lips and gazed up at Marsh House.
The boy with the blond hair and the girl
in the bonnet stared back at him from
a window.

Then they shimmered away into
nothing.

If you have enjoyed this book, why not try these other creepy titles:

The Ghost Bus by Anthony Masters

When Jack and Tina catch a late bus home from school, they realise that something is wrong. This bus is very old-fashioned, but what really gives them a fright is the passengers – they can see right through them. They're on a ghost bus, a ghost bus with a mission...

The Haunted Lighthouse by Anthony Masters

Local people believe that when the seals gather on Black Dog rocks, there'll be a shipwreck. And from the top chamber of the disused lighthouse, Philip can see the seals crowding the rocks below. He hears the eerie sound of footsteps on the staircase and a ghostly figure appears, while outside a storm is brewing and a ship is in danger...

Enter at Your Peril by Eleanor Allen

The old house gives David the creeps, and so does the old woman who owns it. So how did he end up being responsible for feeding her mangy, ancient cat? Each evening David is terrified of entering the house with its dark shadows and strange noises. But when the cat goes missing, David has to investigate the cottage further, and makes a horrifying discovery.

Nightwing Towers by Laurence Staig

Something weird is happening in Nightwing Towers. One by one the residents have disappeared until Charlie's great-aunt is the only one left. So Charlie and Freya investigate the top landing, where they discover the mysterious Mr Kube's sinister secret...

Storybooks are available from your local bookshop or can be ordered direct from the publishers. For more information about storybooks write to: *The Sales Department, Macdonald Young Books, 61 Western Road, Hove, East Sussex BN3 1JD.*

PRINTED IN BELGIUM BY
INTERNATIONAL BOOK PRODUCTION